Triffic

You can learn more about the fight to
save rare breeds of farm animals
from becoming extinct by writing to:

**Rare Breeds Survival Trust
National Agriculture Centre
Stoneleigh Park
Warwickshire
CV8 2LG
UK**

PUFFIN BOOKS

Published by the Penguin Group
Penguin Books Ltd, 27 Wrights Lane, London W8 5TZ, England
Penguin Putnam Inc., 375 Hudson Street, New York, New York 10014, USA
Penguin Books Australia Ltd, Ringwood, Victoria, Australia
Penguin Books Canada Ltd, 10 Alcorn Avenue, Toronto, Ontario, Canada M4V 3B2
Penguin Books (NZ) Ltd, 182–190 Wairau Road, Auckland 10, New Zealand

Penguin Books Ltd, Registered Offices: Harmondsworth, Middlesex, England

First published in *Dick King-Smith's Triffic Pig Book* by Victor Gollancz Ltd 1991
This edition published by Victor Gollancz Ltd 1994
Published in Puffin Books 1998
3 5 7 9 10 8 6 4 2

Printed in Hong Kong by Wing King Tong

British Library Cataloguing in Publication Data
A CIP catalogue record for this book is available from the British Library

ISBN 0–141–30134–1

DICK KING-SMITH

A RARE PIG'S TALE

ILLUSTRATED BY
LIZ GRAHAM-YOOLL

PUFFIN BOOKS

Chapter 1

Only One Girl

"Only one girl?" cried Mrs Berkshire in tones of horror.

"'Fraid so," came the unhappy voice of Mrs Tamworth. "The other five are all boys."

"Oh, I am sorry!" said Mrs Berkshire.

For a moment longer she stood, her front trotters resting on top of the wall that separated their two sties, staring into the dark interior where mother and children lay. Then she heaved her bulk back down and addressed her neighbour on the other side, Mrs Gloucester Old-Spots.

"Glossy!" she called.

"What is it, Betty?"

"Teresa Tamworth has farrowed."

"All well, I trust? How many piglets has she?"

"Six. But there's only one girl."

"Oh dear, oh dear!" grunted Mrs Old-Spots,

4

and she made haste, Betty Berkshire could hear, to pass this disturbing piece of news on down the line of pigsties. So that in a matter of moments Molly Middle-White, Sarah Saddleback and Laetitia Large-Black all knew that poor Teresa Tamworth's litter contained—sad to say—only one girl.

"What a shame!" they said, and, "The pity of it!" and there was much tut-tutting and shaking of heavy heads as the five other sows at the Rare Breeds Survival Centre discussed (in low voices) the Tamworth tragedy. A common or garden pig on an ordinary farm might care not at all about the sexes of her newborn children, but for a sow of a Rare Breed it was a very different matter.

Mrs Tamworth's male piglets, the little hogs, were in general merely destined for the butcher, but their sister the gilt, the little female, was precious beyond belief. In due course she would become a mother herself and thus increase the numbers of her kind, making her particular Rare Breed that much less rare.

This was true of all the animals in the Survival Centre, the cows hoping desperately for heifer calves, the sheep for ewe lambs, the mares for filly foals, and the hens for pullets. Only thus could the spectre of extinction, a fate that had already overtaken so many of the old breeds of British livestock, be kept at bay.

And Teresa Tamworth had had only one girl!

"Her first farrow, I believe," said Laetitia Large-Black to Sarah Saddleback, experienced mothers both. "Let us hope she does not overlay any of them."

"Especially the girl," said Sarah. "That would be too dreadful."

Molly Middle-White grunted in sympathy, but she could not keep a look of smug satisfaction off her squashed-in face, for she was nursing a litter of eight, of which six were female.

Meanwhile, back in her sty Teresa lay, deep in straw and thought, suckling her six baby Tamworths. Sandy-red in colour like their mother, they nuzzled greedily at her, none more greedily than the solitary girl who was already shoving her brothers out of the way at the milk bar. Their hunger at last satisfied, they slept, and Teresa got carefully to her feet.

Betty Berkshire's head appeared over the wall.

"Everything all right, dear?" she said.

"Yes," said Teresa.

She sighed deeply.

"If only they could all have been girls," she said.

"Now, now," said Betty briskly. "You mustn't fret. It could happen to any sow."

She needs something to take her mind off it, she said to herself. I know—choosing names. That'll divert her.

"What are you going to call them?" she said.

"I hadn't thought," said Teresa.

"Not that it matters much what you choose for the boys—Tom, Dick or Harry, any old name will do," said Betty. "In fact I shouldn't bother if I was you. But the girl, now that's different. Specially as she's the only one. Be nice to call her something quite out of the ordinary, something no pig has ever been called before."

"Like what?"

"Oh, I don't know—something posh, Hyacinth, Guinevere, Ermintrude, that sort of name."

"I'll think about it," said Teresa.

She thought about it over the next week, while the six little Tamworths grew bigger and stronger, and began to run about the sty and play games. These mostly took the form of mock fights, and the girl, Teresa noticed, easily held her own against any of her brothers.

She's a proper little tomboy, thought Teresa with a mixture of pride and a tinge of regret that her only daughter was not more ladylike. I can't possibly call her by any of the sort of names Betty suggested. Maybe I'd better let her choose her own name. I'll ask her.

"Children!" she called, and when they all came rushing up she said, "Now you boys go and play quietly in the straw for a little while. I have something to say to your sister."

"Tell her not to be so rough, Mum," said one of the little hogs. "She's always beating us up."

"Girls didn't ought to be like that," said another.

"Girls *ought not* to be like that," said Teresa automatically.

"That's right!" they all shouted. "You tell her, Mum!" and they ran off grumbling.

"Wimps!" said the little gilt scornfully.

"Listen, dear," said Teresa. "I think it's time you had a proper name. It doesn't matter so much with the others, I can just say 'Boys!' if I want to call them, but since you're the only girl, I think it would be nice if you had a name of your own."

"Triffic!" said the little gilt.

"Would you like that?"

"Triffic!"

"Perhaps you'd like to choose your own name?" said Teresa.

"But Mum, I don't know any names."

"Well, shall I choose for you?"

"Yes! Triffic!" said the little gilt again.

How fond of that word she seems to be, thought Teresa, and then suddenly Betty Berkshire's words came into her mind. 'Call her something quite out of the ordinary, something no pig has ever been called before.'

Triffic Tamworth! It had quite a ring to it.

"You've given me an idea," she said, and she shoved her long ginger snout against the piglet's ear and whispered.

"Weeeee!" squealed the little gilt, and she ran at the biggest of her brothers and knocked him flying.

"What are you playing at?" he gasped, and, "Who do you think you are?" cried the other four hogs, and loudly and proudly their only sister answered, "I'm Triffic, I am!"

Late that afternoon, when the pigman came to give the sows their evening meal, he threw open the door of Teresa Tamworth's sty—for she was first in line—and, while the piglets played around his feet, he said, as always, "All right, old lady?"

The pigman called all the sows 'old lady', whether they were young like Teresa, middle-aged like Betty Berkshire, Sarah Saddleback, Glossy Old-Spots and Laetitia Large-Black, or actually elderly like Molly Middle-White.

"I have no idea what you are saying, my good man," grunted Teresa. "And it's a pity you're too stupid to understand me. I could have told you about my daughter's new name."

The pigman poured the food into the trough, and then, as always, he checked on the piglets, counting them on the thick fingers of his large horny hand.

"Only five?" he said. "And them all hogs too? Oh no, old lady—don't tell me you've been and gone and overlaid that little gilt of yours!"

Chapter 2

Octavius

Teresa watched, puzzled, as the pigman
hastened into the inner part of the sty and
searched anxiously through the straw.
Counting was not her strong point, and she
noticed nothing amiss until one of the hogs
said, "She's gone."

"Who's gone?" asked Teresa.

"Wotsername," said another.

"Gone? Where?" said Teresa.

"Out through the door," said the third.

"The man left it open," said the fourth hog.

"Good riddance," said the fifth.

"Can't understand it," said the pigman,
coming out again, and then he saw that he had
indeed left the sty door slightly ajar.

"Little madam!" he said. "She's done a bunk!"
and he hurried out, bolting the door behind
him.

Betty Berkshire's head appeared above the wall.

"What's all the fuss about, dear?" she asked.

"Oh Betty!" said Teresa. "She's gone!"

"Who has?"

"My daughter! My only daughter! She's run away from home. That stupid pigman left the door open and she must have slipped out. Oh dear, oh dear, what am I to do? She's only little, and goodness knows what dangers she may run into out there!"

"Calm yourself, Teresa!" said Betty Berkshire. "So long as she is not trodden on by a bull, or kicked by a cart-horse, or squashed by a tractor, she will be quite all right. I will pass the word along the sties to keep an eye out for her. Have you named her yet?"

"Yes."

"What?"

"Triffic."

"Ah. Hum. Certainly original," said Betty. "Now you just try to relax, dear. A trouble shared is a trouble halved," and off she went to tell the tidings to Glossy and Sarah and Laetitia and Molly.

13

In a remarkably short space of time almost every animal in the Rare Breeds Survival Centre had heard, on the grapevine, the news of the escape. This rapid spread, of fact or of rumour, was, as always, thanks to the pigeons. In the middle of the Centre's great cobbled yard, flanked by the pigsties, the stables, the cattle-courts and the sheep-pens, stood an ancient dovecot shaped like a giant pepper-pot, in which lived a flock of white fantail pigeons. These birds flew freely about the place, scavenging their food from others' leavings and listening with interest to their gossip. One that was preening itself upon a pigsty wall overheard a conversation between Mrs Large-Black and old Mrs Middle-White, and flew back to the dovecot to spread the word.

Within half an hour it was generally known that a very small Tamworth piglet by the name of Triffic was on the loose, and all eyes were on the lookout for her.

Triffic however was nowhere to be seen.

When first she had nipped out of the sty, she had run and run as fast as her short legs would carry her, from sheer excitement at being free, with no four walls to enclose her and no five wimpish brothers to annoy her. She had run right across the wide cobbled yard, empty of people, for the day's parties of visitors to the Survival Centre had by now all gone home. On the far side she saw an open stable door and

dashed inside. Hardly had she flopped down on the floor to catch her breath when she heard a voice.

"Go away, rat," the voice said in deep and mournful tones, "or I'll kick your head off."

Triffic looked up to see a tall grey animal standing at the back of the stable with his rump towards her. He was tethered to a ring fixed in the wooden manger, and now turned his head to look round.

A bony Roman-nosed head it was, with long

splayed ears above it, and the look on the creature's face was melancholy in the extreme. Triffic had no idea what kind of animal it was, but of one thing she was quite certain.

"Excuse me," she said, "but I am *not* a rat. I am a pig. And what's more, I am a Rare Breed of pig."

"Oh, spare us all that guff, do," said the tall grey animal. "That's all they keep on about in this place nowadays, pigs, cattle, sheep, goats, poultry, they're all the same—Rare Breed this and Rare Breed that, makes me sick." He stamped a hind foot loudly on the floor and pulled a wisp of hay from the rack above his head.

Grumpy old thing, thought Triffic. He can't be Rare from the sound of things but then I don't even know what sort of animal he is. Is he a horse perhaps?

"Are you a horse?" she said.

"My poor mother was," said the grey beast dolefully.

"But you're not?"

"No."

"But if your mother was a horse and your father was a horse, you must be a horse too?"

"My father was a donkey."

"I don't get it," said Triffic.

"I am a mule."

"Oh," said Triffic, puzzled. "I am a Tamworth," she said. "My name's Triffic. What's yours?"

The mule swallowed his mouthful of hay and turned around as far as his halter would allow to look down at the piglet.

"Octavius," he said.

"Sorry?"

The mule sighed deeply.

"Octavius, young miss," he said, "is my name. And before you ask any more questions I will tell you that I am the oldest inhabitant of this so-called Rare Breeds Survival Centre. Which when I was a youngster was an ordinary farm. Except that the farmer of those days did not care for noisy smelly great tractors but preferred to work his land with horses. And not only with horses, but with a team of eight mules. Of which I was the youngest. Hence Octavius."

Triffic looked bewildered.

The mule sighed again.

"I am the sole survivor of that team," he said. "I am very old. I spend a lot of my time alone in this dark stable, alone with my memories of my seven dead mates and of the days of long ago. I have no visitors but the stockman and no company but the rats."

He gave a feeble husky bray, halfway between a groan and a cough, and his long floppy ears flopped even further.

"I have no friends," he said.

How miserable he looks, thought Triffic, and quickly she said, "I'll be your friend, Octavius. If you would like."

At that moment a pigeon alighted in the doorway of the stable and waddled up to the piglet, its white tail fanned out behind it.

"You called Triffic?" it said.

"Yes."

"Talk about needles in haystacks," said the pigeon. "We've been looking everywhere for you. Your mother's in a proper state about you. You'd better get off home," and it flew away back towards the pigsties to break the news.

Triffic waited a moment for Octavius to respond to her offer of friendship, but the old mule merely pulled down another mouthful of hay and munched moodily, his grey back towards her and his tufted bell-pull of a tail hanging limp and listless.

"Goodbye then, Octavius," she said, but he made no answer, so she scampered off back across the yard again.

As she neared the line of pigsties she could see first that there were a number of pigeons strutting along the walls, gobbling and cooing, and second, that as a result all her mother's neighbours were standing resting their trotters on their gates and looking out. And all of them, as she passed, expressed their opinions of this runaway child. No piglet of theirs, they all felt sure, would dream of behaving in such a manner.

"Disgraceful!" grunted Laetitia Large-Black

as Triffic passed her sty, and, "Scandalous!" sniffed Sarah Saddleback.

"Worrying your poor mother like that!" grumbled Molly Middle-White, and, "You should be ashamed of yourself!" growled Glossy Old-Spots.

Betty Berkshire merely snorted, but it was a very eloquent snort.

Only Teresa Tamworth was not upon her

gate, because that position was already occupied, by the pigman, looking in.

"Try not to worry, old lady," he was saying as Triffic trotted up behind him. "I've searched everywhere for your little girl but I can't find where she's got to."

And inside, though she understood not a word of this, Teresa was saying, "My little girl's on her way home, you stupid fellow, I've just heard. Get off that gate and look about you."

Which, though her grunts meant nothing to him, the pigman did.

Then he saw Triffic.

Then he gave a great gasp of relief.

Then he opened the door and let her in.

"Well I never, old lady!" he cried. "What have you got to say about that?"

Teresa Tamworth had a great deal to say.

Like any mother who has been worried stiff about her child, she felt a mixture of thankfulness and anger, and no one listening, as the other sows all were, could have guessed at her delight that her daughter was safe and sound.

"Naughty, bad, wicked, thoughtless girl!" she

stormed. "Only a week old and you go gallivanting about just as you please instead of staying here with me. Why can't you be good and well-behaved like your brothers?"

Triffic did not answer, but the five little hogs looked smug, and the listening sows nodded their heavy heads in approval.

"You are never to run away again," said Teresa. "Do you understand?"

"Yes, Mum," said Triffic.

But don't expect me to stay cooped up in this boring old sty with my snotty little brothers, she thought. For one thing, I'm jolly well going to see poor old Octavius again. And I've got a lot more exploring to do yet.

"I won't run away again, Mum," she said.

I'll walk away instead, she thought.

Chapter 3

A Comical Pair

In fact another whole week passed before Triffic
was able to walk away, for the pigman was now

extremely careful about shutting the sty door at feeding times.

Even then it was a matter of luck.

Each morning, before his breakfast, the Manager of the Survival Centre liked to have a wander round and a good look at all the animals in his charge, before the public were admitted.

As it happened, he arrived at the line of sties as the pigman was mucking out Teresa Tamworth, and he leaned on the outer wall, looking in.

"All right, Joe?" he said.

"Yes, Boss," said the pigman. "She's doing 'em well."

"Only one gilt, I think you said?"

"Yes, Boss. Little madam. Look at her now."

The Manager looked, and saw that though the five hogs were frisking around their mother as the pigman swept and shovelled with cries of

"Move over, old lady!" the solitary gilt was waiting by the sty door, peering out through the narrow gap between door and hanging post. She looked alert and tense, like a sprinter waiting in the blocks.

"What's she up to?" asked the Manager.

"Wants to do a bunk, doesn't she," said the pigman. "Done one a week ago. I never shut the door proper, truth to tell, and she slipped out. Gone a good hour she was, Lord knows where, I looked all over."

"How did you get her back?"

"She come of her own accord," said the pigman. "Little madam," and he disappeared into the inner part of the sty, shovel in hand.

The Manager walked round to the door and looked over. The piglet looked up at him. The expression in her eyes, he thought, was knowing.

Grinning like a naughty boy, the Manager opened the door a little, expecting the piglet to rush out, and surprised to see that she walked slowly away up the yard. He bolted the door again and followed at a distance, and saw the piglet, still walking in a leisurely manner, disappear into the stable that housed

Octavius the mule.

"Hullo, Octavius," said Triffic. "I'm back."

"Yes, I would like that," said Octavius in his gloomy voice.

"Like what?"

"I would like to have you for a friend, young miss," said the old grey mule, continuing their last conversation as if no time had elapsed, though in fact Triffic had doubled her age since then.

"Oh brill!" said Triffic. "I'll come and visit you often."

"Do they let you out of your sty then?" asked Octavius.

"The pigman won't, but just now another man actually opened the door for me."

"What did he look like?"

"Tall and thin, with a lot of hair on the bottom of his face."

Standing by the stable door, out of their sight but listening, the Manager stroked his beard reflectively. He could not of course understand a word, but he could hear the piglet grunting away and the soft snickering noises that the mule made in reply. Peeping round, he saw that they were almost nose to nose, the mule's head bent to the piglet's snout.

I've never seen old Octavius appear so relaxed, almost happy, he thought. Not that he's capable of looking really happy, but he actually seems to have found a friend at last, grumpy old thing.

What a comical pair they make! Anyone would think they were talking to one another!

"That must have been the Boss that let you out," said Octavius. "The stockman, that looks after me, he's a small chap with bow legs."

Even as he said this, a small man appeared at the top of the yard and walked, bow-legged, towards the mule's stable.

"Morning, Boss," he said as he approached. "Just going to take Octavius down to the water tank for a drink."

The Manager held a finger to his lips.

"Quiet a minute, Jim," he said softly. "Have a look in here."

When the stockman saw the odd couple, he took off his greasy old cap and scratched his head.

"Did you ever?" he said.

They watched in silence for a while.

"Never known the old mule allow another

animal anywhere near him," said the stockman. "Knock the eye out of a fly, he can, crabby old cuss."

And indeed there was a notice on the stable door:

OCTAVIUS
Do not approach this mule, sole survivor of an eight-mule team, too closely.
He kicks.

But now when the stockman entered, Octavius did not lay back his long ears or roll his eyes or show his yellow teeth or stamp a warning hoof, but stood, quiet as an old sheep, while the stockman untied his halter and led him out of the stable.

The Manager stood watching as the bony old mule went clip-clopping down over the cobbles, the little piglet scuttling along at his heels. At the same time he saw a large fat figure come hurrying up the yard, looking anxiously about him. When the pigman saw the odd couple, he took off his greasy old cap and scratched his head.

"Did you ever?" he said.

At the water tank, Octavius drank deeply, and then, his thirst quenched, bent his grey head to his friend, while drips of water fell from his velvety muzzle on to her upturned snout.

"Here comes the pigman, young miss," he said. "I expect it's time you went back to your mother, isn't it?"

"O.K. Octavius," said Triffic. "See you soon."

"I shall look forward to that," said Octavius, and they touched noses, before Triffic turned and trotted on down to the sties, the pigman following.

All the sows were standing up against their doors, the Manager could see, while the fantail pigeons fluttered excitedly about them, and he could hear the loud angry grunting of the Tamworth as she was reunited with her truant child.

"Don't be too hard on her, Teresa," he said out loud. "You may be Rare, but I suspect that piglet of yours is even rarer. The star attraction of the Survival Centre, that's what she's going to be," and off he went to his breakfast, of fried bacon, from a common or garden pig, that had not survived.

Chapter 4

Mules Can't

The Manager knew that a great many of the
visitors to the Survival Centre were children,
either with their parents or in a school party.
He knew also that most children love animals,
especially a baby animal such as a piglet, and
particularly, without doubt, a small ginger
piglet that, of all unlikely things, had struck up
a friendship with a large grey mule. Already he
had high hopes of Triffic as a crowd-puller. He
needed to pull in the crowds to get money for
his work of saving Rare Breeds.

"Joe," he said to the pigman next day, "I
want you to let that little Tamworth gilt out,
every morning, as soon as there are enough
visitors around, understand?"

"Yes, Boss," said the pigman, puzzled.

Little madam of a pig, he thought, what's
going on?

And to the stockman the Manager said, "I want Octavius exercised, Jim, every morning, as soon as there are enough visitors around, understand?"

"Yes, Boss," said the stockman, stumped.

Crabby old cuss of a mule, he thought, what's going on?

The sows too wondered what was going on.

Gradually, as the days went by, Teresa grew accustomed to Triffic's little outings and no

longer took her to task. In fact she began to feel
rather proud that a child of hers should be
allowed a privilege that was denied to all other
piglets.

But the rest were none too pleased,
particularly when they learned the truth of the
matter from the gossiping pigeons.

"Walking round the yard with a *mule*!"
grunted Molly Middle-White.

"A mule!" sniffed Laetitia Large-Black. "The

lowest form of animal life!"

"And attracting *crowds* of people!" grumbled Sarah Saddleback.

"Who should be down here admiring *our* children!" growled Glossy Old-Spots.

Even Betty Berkshire, closer to Teresa than the others, could not content herself with a mere snort but must needs comment directly. She looked over the wall one day, when the pigman had just let Triffic back into the sty, and shook her head disapprovingly.

"Naughty little girl!" she said.

Teresa bristled.

"Are you addressing my daughter, Mrs Berkshire?" she said.

"I am," said Betty. "You'll forgive me for saying so, Teresa, speaking as a much older sow, but you are allowing the child to make an exhibition of herself."

"You should just have heard my mum!" said Triffic to Octavius next morning. "'No, Mrs Berkshire,' she said. 'I will not forgive you, and I'll thank you to mind your own pigginess and keep your snout out of mine.' You should have seen the expression on Auntie Betty's face,

Octavius! She was gobsmacked!"

"Your mother sounds a spirited person, young miss," said Octavius.

They were walking round the yard together, the stockman leading the mule and the piglet trotting beside, as the crowd of onlookers oohed and aahed at the sight of the odd couple.

"She is also very fortunate," went on Octavius, "to have such a daughter," and he sighed deeply.

"Have you never had a daughter then?" said Triffic.

"No."

"Only sons?"

"No."

"No children at all?"

"No," said Octavius in his customary tones of deepest gloom. "Mules can't."

"Can't have children of their own?" said Triffic. "Not ever?"

"That's right."

They went on in silence for a while. Then Octavius said, "It used not to bother me, but since meeting you, young miss, I have often wished that I could have had a child of my own."

Poor old chap, thought Triffic, and then she had an idea.

"Tell you what," she said. "I haven't got a father—at least I have, but not here, I've never seen him. He lives at another Survival Centre, Mum told me—she went over there for the wedding. So you could be my adopted father, Octavius. Then you'd have a daughter as well as a friend."

Octavius stopped abruptly in his tracks and stood stock-still. Unbreakably stubborn like all his kind, he took no notice of the stockman's efforts to haul him forward again, but with a sudden jerk of his head twitched the end of the halter-rope from the man's hands.

"Young miss," he said, "you have just made an old mule very happy. They named you well when they called you Triffic."

At these words Triffic also felt very happy. Without really thinking what she was doing, she took the end of the rope in her mouth and walked on. Octavius followed.

"Look at that!" cried somebody in the crowd of watching visitors, and everyone, the children especially, looked and pointed and laughed and cheered at the amazing sight of a very old grey mule being led around the cobbled yard of the Survival Centre by a very young ginger piglet.

The pigman came up to see what all the noise was about, and stood beside the stockman.

"Did you ever, Jim?" he said.

"I never, Joe," said the stockman, and they took off their greasy old caps and scratched their heads.

Next morning the Manager, forewarned by his men, came to watch.

He stood beside Joe and saw Jim drop the

rope and the piglet once again pick up the end of it and walk on. He listened to the delighted comments of the day's visitors.

"What a wonderful pair!" they said, and, "It's better than a circus!" and, "Ought to be on the telly, they did!" and he stroked his beard and smiled behind his hand.

"You know what, Joe?" he said to the pigman. "She's terrific, she is!"

The weeks passed, weeks in which larger and larger numbers of people came to visit the Centre, to see now, in addition to all the Rare Breeds of cattle and horses and sheep and pigs and goats and poultry, the daily show put on in the great yard by old Octavius and his little friend.

By now the act was improved, thanks to an idea of the Manager's.

Experimenting with the pair one evening after the public had gone home, he found that when he ordered Octavius to stop, the piglet had perforce to do so also, since patently she could not tow the mule forward: and when he told Octavius to go on again, so must Triffic or risk being stepped on.

So now to the visitors' delight the word "Whoa!" brought both to a halt, and then away they both went again at the command "Walk on!"

"What was all that noise I heard just now?" said Teresa when Triffic returned after the first demonstration of these new skills.

"That was the people, Mum," said Triffic. "They were cheering Octavius and me like anything, can't think why. Funny creatures, people. Make an awful row about nothing, they do, just like my brothers."

She looked round the outer part of the sty.

"By the way, where are they?" she said. "All asleep inside?"

"No," said Teresa. "They've gone."

"Gone? Where?"

"I don't know," said Teresa (who didn't).

Next door Betty Berkshire (who did) gave a loud snort. She said nothing however, since she and Teresa were still not on speaking terms.

The pigman came in with a bucket and filled the trough.

"There you are, old lady, eat up and get your

strength back, got to have you in good condition ready for the next lot," he said. "And as for you, little madam, you're on your own now. I expect you'll miss your brothers, eh?"

"What's he on about, Mum?" said Triffic.

"Haven't a clue," said Teresa. "I expect you'll miss your brothers, eh?"

"You must be joking, Mum," said Triffic with her mouth full. "There's no one to hog my grub any more."

Chapter 5

She's Moved House

Leading Octavius around the yard and stopping and starting on command were soon not the only tricks in Triffic's repertoire.

All pigs are intelligent and Triffic, it seemed, was especially so for she quickly learned a number of other bits of business which the Manager thought up to amuse the public.

All of them demanded the co-operation of Octavius, hitherto the most unco-operative animal anyone could imagine, but now, to the stockman's great surprise, eager to please.

He stood still when told, for example, and let the piglet walk between his legs. He lay down flat on his side so that she could play King of the Castle upon his stomach. He even allowed himself to be harnessed to a kind of sledge, upon which the Manager trained Triffic to stand, and pulled her along behind him. And all this the old mule did willingly, with never even the threat of the biting and kicking that once was his stock-in-trade.

"Can't understand it, Boss," the stockman said. "No one would ever believe what a crabby old cuss he was. He's a changed animal."

The Manager nodded. He understood Octavius's altered state only too well, and he blamed himself fairly and squarely for having allowed the animal to be tied up in a dark stable all this time, as though he was some sort of pariah. At least this state of affairs had been put right. The old mule had been moved to a fine roomy loose-box whose door bore a notice saying simply:

OCTAVIUS
The sole survivor of
an eight-mule team

And now thanks to Triffic, Octavius had not only a friend (an adopted daughter you might say, the Manager caught himself thinking, smiling at the absurdity of such a notion) but also the daily admiration, adulation indeed, of the crowds who came to watch and applaud the increasingly famous pig-and-mule act. Such was the demand for it that there were now two performances each morning and afternoon.

Triffic worried a bit about this.

"Octavius," she said.

"Yes, my dear."

"You're sure it's not too much for you? Four shows a day, I mean—it's a lot of walking and pulling that sledge and everything. After all, you're not as young as you were."

"On the contrary, my dear," replied Octavius, "I am younger than I was, much younger—in spirit, that is. They feed me better, indeed I even get a ration of oats now, I have a large well-lit new home with room to roll and stretch out comfortably in the straw, I have all the fresh air and exercise that I lacked before, and, to be frank, I must confess that I derive a good deal of enjoyment from performing our little shows, as you call them. It is most pleasant, I find, to be the centre of attention, clapped and cheered by the people. It has taken years off me. And it is all thanks to you, my dear."

Triffic was quite reassured by this long speech from her adopted father, which she later reported to her natural mother.

"He's so much happier, Mum," she said, "you wouldn't believe."

"I am glad for him," said Teresa. "And I am glad for you, child, that you seem to have this gift of spreading happiness. Why, the fantail pigeons tell me that you are given a welcome wherever you go in the Centre—from the biggest Longhorn bull to the smallest bantam hen. Certainly my neighbours have nothing but good to say of you now."

This change of heart on behalf of the other sows was easily explained. Each time that Triffic finished her act and ran home, a great many of the visitors, the children especially, followed her down to the line of pigsties, and so paid far more attention than ever before to the rest of the Rare mother and baby pigs.

"You'd never think to look at them," people said, staring down at the sows and their litters, "that they were so intelligent. But they must be—just look what that little ginger one has learned to do."

"You'd never think to look at them," grunted Molly Middle-White, staring up at the people, "that they had much in the way of brains. But they must have—just look at them admiring our children."

"They follow that Triffic Tamworth down here, I notice," said Laetitia Large-Black.

"That's true," said Sarah Saddleback. "She seems to attract them in this direction."

"At least she's making herself useful," said Glossy Old-Spots.

"Maybe we misjudged her," said Betty Berkshire. She looked over the wall and nodded her head approvingly.

"Good little girl!" she said.

"Who, me, Auntie Betty?" said Triffic.

"Yes, you, dear."

"I'm glad that you seem to approve of my daughter now, Betty," said Teresa drily.

"Oh yes," said Betty Berkshire. "Let bygones be bygones, that's my motto. Life's too short."

Or it is for some pigs, she thought. Thank goodness I was born a female and of a Rare Breed.

"I expect it's quite a relief to be rid of your hogs, Teresa," she said. "A first litter is always tiring. And the way time flies, you'll be hearing the patter of tiny trotters again before you can look round. You'll be wanting young Triffic out of the way then."

"She's welcome to stay as long as she likes," said Teresa Tamworth.

Triffic saw her opportunity. For some time now she had been growing impatient of her dependence upon the pigman coming to let her out or in, and of her imprisonment in the sty at times when she was not performing. What she wanted was total freedom to go wherever she liked whenever she liked within the Rare Breeds Survival Centre. More, she fancied sharing Octavius's loose-box—an easy matter since the stockman had fixed rails across the front of it upon which the public could lean to look at the mule and under which Triffic could easily go.

"Mum," she said now. "Would you mind awfully if I moved in with my friend Octavius?"

Teresa hesitated. She was fond of this child, her first and so far only daughter, but she was aware that, as Betty said, there would be other daughters and sons before too long. Besides, some instinct told her that Triffic was a very special individual, destined for great things, so at length she answered her question quite simply.

"Of course not, my love," she said. "You go and keep your old mule company. But come back for a chat now and again, won't you?"

"Oh yes," said Betty. "You must come and see us all. You're such a crowd-puller, you know."

"I will!" said Triffic. "Every day."

Later, after the second afternoon performance, the pigman had finished feeding the sows and was leaning on Teresa's door, waiting for Triffic.

"Where's that little madam got to then, old lady?" he said when the piglet did not appear, but Teresa only grunted. So the pigman walked up the yard till he saw the stockman coming out of Octavius's loose-box.

"Seen my Tamworth gilt, Jim?" he said.

"That I have, Joe," said the stockman, and he jerked his thumb over his shoulder.

"Take a look," he said.

The pigman took it. There was Octavius lying comfortably in his deep bed of straw, and beside him lay Triffic.

She jumped up when she saw the pigman and let out a string of little snorts and squeaks that said plainly, "I'm hungry, you stupid fellow, so kindly fetch a trough and some food to put in it, and look sharp!"

When the pigman had obeyed—for even he could not misinterpret this message—he and the stockman leaned upon the rails, elbows on the upper one, a foot each on the lower, and stared thoughtfully at the odd couple. They did not take off their greasy caps to scratch their heads, because by now they were thoroughly used to the partnership, and both knew, for the Manager had told them, how important it had become. Never had the takings been so good, especially since the media had cottoned on to the double act and given the Centre so much publicity. Only recently a television crew had come to record the latest trick which the Manager had devised.

He fitted Octavius, harnessed to the sledge with a set of reins, and those parts which a human driver would normally have held he coated with treacle. Then he trained Triffic to hold them in her mouth. This, having a lot of very sweet teeth, she willingly did, and the nation's TV screens showed the astounding sight of a piglet not merely being pulled along by a mule, but actually driving one.

"Reckon she's moved house then, Jim," said the pigman. Little madam, he was about to say but somehow that no longer seemed right.

"Little marvel!" he said.

"Reckon you're right, Joe," said the stockman. "The old mule won't half be pleased, though you'd never think so to look at him." Crabby old cuss, he was about to add but somehow that no longer seemed right.

"Funny old codger!" he said.

The little marvel and the funny old codger settled down most happily together. Octavius was never now lonely for one moment, and as for Triffic, though she liked to potter about all over the Centre, chatting to this animal and that, and never forgetting regular visits to her

mother and her aunties, she most looked
forward to the end of the working day. Then she
could settle down in the loose-box and listen to
all the tales that Octavius had to tell, of the
days of long ago.

He spoke of his father the donkey and his
mother the mare, and of his seven mates in the
eight-strong team. Primus, the eldest, had once
been an army mule, carrying heavy machine-
guns up Italian mountains, and Quartus and
Quintus had worked in a circus, "but the best
times, my dear," said Octavius, "was when all
eight of us were employed together, here on the
farm. Forget your Shire horses and your
Percherons and your Suffolk Punches—there
was no load so heavy that we lads couldn't shift
it. What a bunch of boys we were. All gone now
though, except me, and I dare say I shan't be
long in following them."

"Oh rubbish, Octavius," said Triffic. "There's
no danger of that."

But there was.

Late one afternoon, just before closing time,
when the last of the day's visitors were leaving the
Survival Centre, four people were still standing

at the front of Octavius's loose-box. A man and a woman leaned on the top rail, their two children on the bottom, staring at the piglet and the mule.

The children were eating sweets, and the man was puffing a cigarette despite the NO SMOKING notice on the loose-box door as on every other door of the Centre, where so much hay and straw were stored.

They were not cruel people, just thoughtless, and the children chucked their sweet-papers and the bag that had held the toffees on the floor, despite the fact that one of the many bins labelled LITTER was handy.

"Time to go," said the man to his wife, and he took a final puff and dropped his fag-end, and off they all went.

The butt of the cigarette lay on the cobbles, still glowing. Then a little breeze blew in through the door and shifted the sweet-bag towards it. It caught alight. The paper bag lay burning and might have burned out had not the little breeze blown in once more, and lifted it, and moved it, just a couple of feet.

But that was enough to drop it on to the edge of Octavius's straw bed.

Chapter 6

A Heroine

Those last four visitors (the man just lighting another cigarette) were in the act of walking out of the main gates of the Centre as the outer edge of Octavius's bed caught fire.

His day's work done, the pigman was having a last look down the line of sties, and the stockman, in the main stables, was giving a final friendly slap to the gleaming black backside of a great Shire stallion before knocking off.

In his office, the Manager stroked his beard contentedly as his secretary told him the total of the day's takings and as he converted, in his head, the sum of money into bales of hay and bags of concentrates to feed his beloved Rare Breeds.

Octavius was in the middle of a story about Secundus, the strongest mule of the team, who had once been hitched to a cow that had slipped into a deep ditch and had hauled her out by his own unaided efforts.

At that moment the flames took a proper hold of the thick dry straw, and rose in an almost solid wall along the line of the rails across the front of the loose-box.

"Quick!" groaned the old grey mule, backing hastily away from the blaze. "Get out while you can!"

Triffic dashed to safety beneath the bottom rail, at the far end, where the flames had not yet reached. She turned to see them reach it. There was a side-door to the loose-box, she knew, but it was bolted, and the mule was too big to get under or between the rails and too old and stiff to be able to jump out.

The first thought that Triffic had was to get help, and the last thing she heard, as she ran squealing at the top of her voice down the yard, was the frantic battering of Octavius's heels as he tried to kick down the rails.

The pigman heard the earsplitting non-stop row the piglet was making, and looked up, and saw the smoke. He grabbed a couple of buckets and ran for the water tank as fast as his bulk would allow.

The stockman too heard the noise and saw the smoke. He unreeled the stable hosepipe and ran for the loose-box as fast as his bow legs would let him.

Both men yelled "FIRE! FIRE!" and the Manager heard them from his office.

"Nine Nine Nine! Fire Brigade! Quick!" he snapped at his secretary, and he snatched an extinguisher off the wall.

He could hear the crackle of flames as he raced across the yard, and because he was fit and long-legged he arrived at the same time as his men. Flinging them the extinguisher, he dashed around to the side-door of the loose-box.

Triffic watched all this, her heart thudding madly. There was no sound from within now, nothing but the roar of the fire. A horse trapped thus would have been screaming, but a mule will bear terrible pain and make no sound. Triffic did not know this fact. He's dead, she said to herself.

Then, as the Manager drew the bolt of the side-door, she saw, to her immense relief, Octavius totter out. He was shaking like a leaf, she could see, and the tuft on the end of his bell-pull tail had been scorched off, but he was safe!

By the time the fire engine arrived, the three men had the fire under control, and all that remained was for the firemen to play their hoses on neighbouring buildings to damp them down.

Things could have been much worse.

The rails had burned, the wooden manger too, and Octavius's tack, hung on the blackened walls, was ruined. But the roof was undamaged, and everything could be put right again.

Only the Manager saw that by a strange chance the flames that had licked at the notice

on the open front door had done so selectively.
Now it simply read:

"Things could have been much worse," he said
to Joe and Jim, when the fire brigade had left.

"We'd have been too late, Boss," the stockman
said, "if it hadn't been for Joe's little Tamworth."

"Jim's right," said the pigman. "If she hadn't
made all that racket we'd never have noticed in
time. Saved the old mule's life, she did."

"And a lot more lives too, I dare say," said the
Manager, brushing bits of blackened straw out
of his beard. "If that fire had really taken hold,
it would have run right down the line of
buildings, Dutch barn and all. The Centre
would have been pretty well ruined. She's a
heroine, that piglet is, and I'll make sure the
newspapers hear all about it. Just look at the
pair of them now."

The three men looked down the yard, where Octavius, still trembling, was taking a long drink. Then, his thirst quenched, he bent his grey head to his friend, while drips of water fell from his velvety muzzle on to her upturned snout.

"Thank you, my dear little girl," he said simply, and they rubbed noses.

Some weeks passed before Triffic and Octavius could put on their act again. The old mule needed a rest to recover from the shock, the Manager thought, and anyway the tack had to be replaced, and the sledge, which had also burned.

Meanwhile the loose-box had to be put to rights again and thoroughly cleaned, the walls whitewashed, and the rails and manger replaced.

No one knew for sure what had caused the fire, but there was little doubt in the Manager's mind, and he had a large new notice made and posted by the main gates, which said:

SMOKING IS STRICTLY PROHIBITED ANYWHERE IN THE CENTRE. YOUR CARELESSLY DROPPED CIGARETTE ENDS COULD COST THE LIVES OF THESE ANIMALS. WE WANT OUR RARE BREEDS TO SURVIVE. PLEASE DO NOT SMOKE

Everyone knew, through newspapers and television, of the fire and of the heroic part that the piglet had played (as indeed did all the animals in the Centre, for the pigeons told them), and everyone was waiting eagerly to see the odd couple perform once again. But in the meantime, something else happened.

Triffic went down to the pigsties one morning to say hello to her mother, and was surprised to find the Tamworth's sty besieged by a crowd.

There was nothing unusual about the sows attracting attention—lots of people came to admire old Molly with her squashed-in face, or the gleaming blackness of Laetitia, or Sarah's saddle, or Glossy's spots, or dark-brown Betty Berkshire with her white forehead and feet and her double chin. But why, this day, was everyone pushing and shoving for a look into one sty only—that of the sandy-red long-snouted Teresa Tamworth?

Triffic stood behind the feet of the jostling crowd, wondering what on earth was happening.

Just then two fantails flew down from the old pepper-pot-shaped dovecot and began to peck around at bits of food that people had dropped.

"What's up?" said Triffic. "Is my Mum all right?"

"She's all right and no mistake," said one of the pigeons.

"Haven't you heard?" said the second pigeon.

"No, what?"

"Happy event," said the first bird.

"Seven happy events," said the other.

"Two boys . . . "

" . . . and five girls."

Triffic ran to find Octavius.

"What d'you think!" she squealed excitedly.
"I've got two brothers and *five* sisters! Oh
Octavius, won't Mum be pleased!"

That evening when all the visitors had gone,
Triffic went down to the yard again and stood
outside her mother's door.

"Mum!" she called.

"What is it dear," said Teresa. "I'm rather
busy."

"But Mum, can't I have a look at the new
babies?"

"Not just now."

"Later then?"

"We'll see."

"Run along, Triffic, there's a good girl," said Betty Berkshire from next door. "Your mother doesn't want to be bothered."

"Mum doesn't want to be bothered with me any more, Octavius," said Triffic that night.

"It's natural," said Octavius. "All her concern is for her new litter." He gave his feeble bray, half cough, half groan.

"You mustn't be sad about it," he said, "or you will make me feel sad again and that would never do."

"It certainly wouldn't," said Triffic.

She looked at her friend's face, set as usual in an expression of extreme melancholy.

"You *are* happy, Octavius, aren't you?" she said.

"I am, my dear," said the old mule. "So long as I have you."

And he was happier still a couple of days later when they moved back into the renovated loose-box. New tack had been bought, a new sledge constructed, and then, after a period of rehearsals, they were ready for the opening performance, the first since the fire.

The pigman had groomed Triffic with great care, oiling her ginger hair and even cleaning and polishing her trotters.

As for Octavius, the stockman had brushed and curry-combed him till his grey coat shone. His long ears, as usual, would not stand up properly, his upright mane was too short to do much with, and the hair on his tail-tassel had not yet fully grown back, but all the same he looked in fine fettle for such an old fellow. It was hard to remember now that bony despondent-looking wreck upon which Triffic Tamworth had first set eyes.

What a crowd turned up that morning! The great cobbled yard of the Survival Centre was packed with people, clapping and cheering as Triffic and Octavius went through their act.

The Manager stood watching the finale—the driving of Octavius by Triffic, the treacle-smeared reins held in her mouth—and the very latest trick he had taught her—to get off the sledge and then go down on her knees in a last bow to the crowd.

She performed it perfectly, and he stroked his beard and listened to the roars of applause.

Just in front of him a small boy was jumping up and down and shouting with excitement.

"Did you enjoy it?" he said to him.

"Yes!" cried the boy. "It's great! What's his name, mister?"

"Octavius," said the Manager.

"That's a funny name."

"Well, you see, he's the survivor of an eight-mule team."

"No," said the boy. "I don't mean the mule. I mean the pig. What's his name?"

"It isn't a he," said the Manager. "It's a she. And actually, she hasn't got a name."

"She's *triffic*!" said the boy. "That's what she is!"

"O.K." said the Manager. "You said it. She's Triffic."